Early Sunday Morning

Early Sunday Morning

DENENE MILLNER

ILLUSTRATED BY VANESSA BRANTLEY-NEWTON

A Denene Millner Book

Simon & Schuster Books for Young Readers
New York   London   Toronto   Sydney   New Delhi

SIMON & SCHUSTER BOOKS FOR YOUNG READERS

An imprint of Simon & Schuster Children's Publishing Division

1230 Avenue of the Americas, New York, New York 10020

Previously published in 2017 by Bolden Books, an imprint of Agate Publishing

SIMON & SCHUSTER BOOKS FOR YOUNG READERS is a trademark of Simon & Schuster, Inc.

For information about special discounts for bulk purchases, please contact Simon & Schuster Special

Sales at 1-866-506-1949 or business@simonandschuster.com.

The Simon & Schuster Speakers Bureau can bring authors to your live event.

For more information or to book an event, contact the Simon & Schuster

Speakers Bureau at 1-866-248-3049 or visit our website at www.simonspeakers.com.

Book design by Morgan Krehbiel

The text for this book was set in Playtime With Hot Toddies.

This illustrations for this book were sketched in pencil and then colored digitally.

Manufactured in China

0120 SCP

First Simon & Schuster Books for Young Readers hardcover edition May 2020

10 9 8 7 6 5 4 3 2 1

Library of Congress Cataloging-in-Publication Data

Names: Millner, Denene, author. | Brantley-Newton, Vanessa, illustrator.

Title: Early Sunday morning / Denene Millner ; illustrated by Vanessa Brantley-Newton.

Description: First edition. | New York : Simon & Schuster Books for Young Readers, 2020. |

Audience: Ages 4-8. | Audience: Grades K-1. | Summary: As she nervously prepares for

her first solo in the church youth choir, June collects helpful advice from family and friends.

Identifiers: LCCN 2019050357 | ISBN 9781534476530 (hardcover) | ISBN 9781534476547 (ebook)

Subjects: CYAC: Anxiety—Fiction. | Singing—Fiction. | Family life—Fiction. |

Church attendance—Fiction. | African Americans—Fiction.

Classification: LCC PZ7.M63957 Ear 2020 | DDC [E]—dc23

LC record available at https://lccn.loc.gov/2019050357

For my mother, Bettye, who taught me how to love God,
and for my father, Jimy, who taught me how to love myself.
That's love. —D. M.

For Mama Shirley, who taught us to sing, pray, and praise,
and to rise early Sunday mornings. —V. B.-N.

Sunday is the Lord's day, when Mommy, Daddy, my brother, and I go to church. This Sunday is extra special because I'll be singing my first solo in the youth choir.

I sing lots of songs in the mirror when no one is watching. Sometimes, Daddy and I sing loud, silly songs together and giggle at the funny words. Singing with Daddy is when I am happiest of all.

But singing by myself with a microphone in
front of a crowd is big. And a little scary.
Even at choir rehearsal when barely anyone is
watching me practice, my voice gets all trembly.

One day, I heard Angela and Tommy whisper and giggle as I walked back to my seat. "Good grief, Sister Sarah could have just given that solo to a goat. It might not remember the words, but at least it would be able to sing the notes." Their words stung. So did my tears.

Everybody knows I am nervous, and so they all tell me their ideas for how I can sing my song strong and clear. Auntie thinks wearing a new dress will help. "Looking fancy makes you feel brave!" she promises.

Even Mr. Harvey, the barber, adds in his two cents. "See, what you have to do is pretend everyone in the audience has a big ol' watermelon head. You'll be too busy laughing to be scared," he says as he spins my brother, Troy, around in the chair.

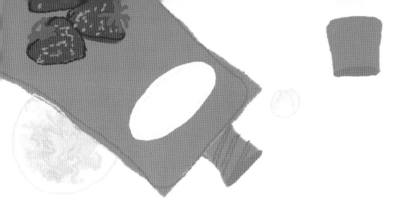

The night before my big solo, Mommy washes my hair with strawberry shampoo and sits me on pillows while she twists it into a beautiful crown.

Sometimes, if I sit really still and don't make too much of a fuss, she lets me have a bowl of ice cream. But I am fidgety. "Tomorrow you'll sing your song so pretty, the angels will shout in Heaven," she says. "Believe that with all your heart."

"I will," I say quietly.

jamais rien
toujours
e petice part ?
abeolument
décaisonnable
las demain

Early Sunday morning is when the magic happens. A gentle nudge and it's rise and shine, give God the glory!

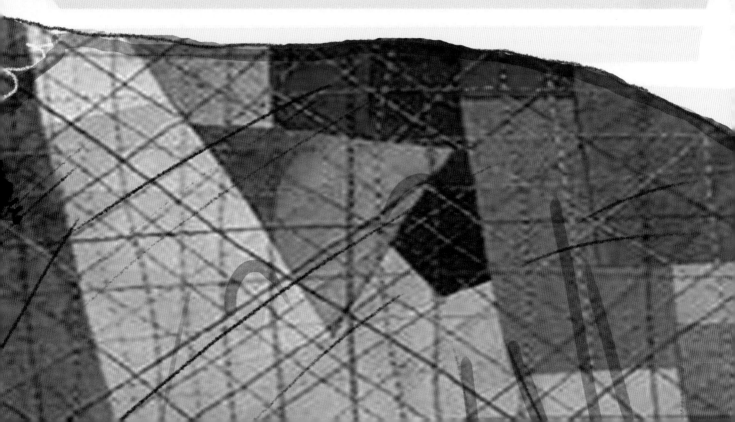

Troy and I wake up to the smell of roast beef, macaroni and cheese, collards, corn bread, and sweet potato pie—my favorite. Mommy always makes Sunday dinner in the morning so we can eat right after church. That's because sometimes, when Pastor Scott gets lost in the rhythm, he can preach on . . . and on . . . and on . . . waaaaay into the afternoon. We eat cereal and toast to hold us over until dinnertime.

After breakfast, I brush my teeth and wash my face and check my hair while Mommy lays out my church clothes: New dress. Tights. And my Mary Janes, shined up like new pennies.

My choir robe hangs from the top of my
bedroom door, stretching like a white river
almost to the doorknob. A sight to see!

Troy steps out of his room cool as you please
in his suit and tie, looking just like Daddy when
he takes Mommy out dancing. He giggles
when he sees me twirling in my fancy dress.

We both watch Mommy swoosh gloss across her lips. When she gives a little tug at her church hat and pinches each of our cheeks, Troy and I know it's almost time to go.

We wake Daddy to hug and kiss him goodbye. He worked an extra shift at the bakery, so on this Sunday, he will have to rest. Daddy won't be coming to see me sing. This makes me sad.

But he gives me peppermints and money for the offering, plus a hug and lots of kisses to help me be brave. "If you get nervous, just pick a spot in the church and sing to it like you do your mirror," he says. "Daddy will be there with you in spirit, singing along with you." Knowing this will have to do.

I can barely keep still in Ms. Ellis's Sunday School class. We're learning about love and how it is patient and kind and never, ever fails. Ms. Ellis's lesson makes me want to hug Mommy and Daddy and Troy and Grandpa Jimy and Grandma Bettye and Belly, our puffy blue angel fish. But then I see the microphone over by the choir pews, and suddenly, I am scared again.

I watch the hands on the clock as the collection plate is passed . . . and Deacon Claytor reads the announcements . . . and little Kelvin makes the whole Sunday School laugh when he prays for God to make Pastor Scott's sermon end early enough for him to watch the football game.

After Sunday School, Mommy helps me into my robe. Then she folds my hands into hers and gives me that knowing look—one that says, "Everything is going to be all right." I want to believe that. At least, I try.

When our youth choir marches through the doors, every eye is on us. We float down the aisle like an army of angels, lifting our voices in praise all the way up to the rafters. And right there at the end of the pew is Mommy, smiling and singing and waving her fan.

I fidget while Pastor Scott welcomes the visitors and leads the prayer. Then the notes to my song rise up from the organ. Ms. Jackson's fingernails tap loudly against the keys as the melody fills the church. "Praise him!" I hear my mother say. "Tell it to the Lord," one of the deaconesses shouts.

I don't look at the choir director or even my mother. I do not imagine watermelons or remember what my dress looks like. Instead, I pick a spot to focus on, just like Daddy told me to, and I lean into the microphone as I stare at the double doors.

And just when I swallow really hard . . .
And take a deep breath . . .
And get ready to sing my first note . . .
The double doors swing open . . .

And there is Daddy, standing tall and
handsome with a smile outshined only by
mine! "Sing, baby," he shouts.

I lift my voice and sing with the might of the angels—just like I do when I'm alone in my room dancing in front of my mirror, and when Daddy is singing alongside me, too.

And the church shouts, "Amen!"